What Happens When I Talk to God?

The Power of Prayer for Boys and Girls

By Stormie Omartian
Artwork by Shari Warren

HARVEST HOUSE PUBLISHERS
EUGENE, OREGON

What Happens When I Talk to God?

Text copyright © 2007 by Stormie Omartian
Artwork copyright © 2007 by Shari Warren. Licensed by Bentley Licensing Group.

Published by Harvest House Publishers
Eugene, OR 97402

ISBN 978-0-7369-1676-9
ISBN 978-0-7369-5885-1 (The 1687 Foundation Edition)

Back cover author photo © Michael Gomez / Gomez Photography

Design and production by Koechel Peterson & Associates, Minneapolis, Minnesota

14 15 16 17 18 / QG / 10 9 8 7 6 5 4 3 2

The 1687 Foundation First Printing, 2013

Printed in the United States of America

This book made available without charge by The 1687 Foundation, a nonprofit, tax-exempt organization dedicated to advancing spiritual and charitable purposes. Please note that these books may only be given away. They cannot be sold, cannot be used to raise money, and cannot be a "free giveaway" for any commercial or personal-gain purpose whatsoever.

For additional information, please contact:
Email: info@1687foundation.com
Tel: 541.549.7600
Fax: 541.549.7603

It's never too soon to teach a child to pray.
—STORMIE OMARTIAN

Talking to God is called prayer. God wants us to talk to Him all the time. That's why I try to talk to Him every day. Sunday, Monday, Tuesday, Wednesday, Thursday, Friday, Saturday—every day is the perfect day to pray!

God likes it when I talk to Him. That's because He loves me and wants to spend time with me. He likes to hear that I love Him too. So when I talk to God, I always tell Him how much I love Him. I say, "I love You, God."

Every time I talk to God, I am getting to know Him better. God wants **every single person** to talk to Him and get to know Him. This is something I can do **every day, wherever** I am.

Another way I can **get to know God** is by reading my Bible or listening to Bible stories. God gave us **His Word**—the Bible—so we can learn more about Him. The Bible tells us how to **pray** and **talk to God.** I say, "Thank You, God, for **the Bible!"**

The Bible says that God wants me to thank Him for all the good things in my life. Having a family who loves me and takes care of me is definitely a good thing!

I can thank God for my mom and dad, brothers and sisters, grandparents and cousins— for everyone in my family! I can also thank God for my friends and for all the people who love me. I say, "Thank You, God, for everyone You have put in my life for me to love."

God wants us to thank Him for all the wonderful things He has given us. So I thank Him for the clear blue sky, soft green grass, and fluffy white clouds. I thank Him for the blowing wind, cool rain, and warm sunshine. I thank Him for big trees and colorful flowers, for high mountains and deep oceans—for everything God made!

I say, "Thank You, God, for giving me healthy food to eat and clean water to drink. Thank You for a warm place to live and a cozy bed to sleep in every night. Thank You for my favorite toys and places I can go to play."

When I pray, I can't wait to thank God for all of the huggable, loveable creatures He has made. I also thank Him for creatures that might not make good pets but are still fun to look at and learn all about—like elephants, giraffes, bears, tigers, eagles, dolphins, and whales. Every animal on land, every fish in the water, and every bird in the sky is a special creation given to us by God.

I say, "Thank You, God, for dogs and cats, horses and rabbits, birds and hamsters—and all animals I can pet and love. Thank You for every wonderful animal You have made."

What is a friend? A friend is someone who talks to you and **cares about you.** God wants me to talk to Him because He is my friend. And friends **always** talk to each other! You can't be friends with someone you never talk to. That's why **talking to God** every day is so important.

My favorite thing about talking to God is that I can talk to Him about **anything.** God wants me to **tell Him** about the things that matter to me. That's because anything I care about, He cares about too! **Whatever** is important to me is also important to God. I say, "Thank You, God, that You are my friend and I can tell You everything."

I can talk to God about good things, but I can talk to Him about bad things too. He wants to know when something makes me happy, and He also wants to know when something makes me sad. That way He can help me!

God always listens to me, and He always understands just how I feel. And I always feel better after I talk to God. I say, "Thank You, God, that I can talk to You about anything."

God always hears me pray no matter where I am. I can talk to Him when I'm under the covers in bed, and He also listens to me when I'm soaking in the bathtub!

I can talk to God when I'm inside playing with my toys or when I'm outside playing ball. He hears me when I'm jumping, running, or walking, or even when I'm sitting somewhere eating ice cream! God hears me when I'm talking to Him standing up or kneeling down or lying in bed. I say, "Thank You, God, that You are always there for me."

God listens to me any time of the day or night. I can talk to Him in the morning after I get up or in the afternoon when I am playing. I can even talk to Him at night when the only light I see comes from the moon and stars.

God likes for me to talk to Him before I eat so I can thank Him for my food. He also loves to hear my bedtime prayers right before I go to sleep. I always thank Him for my day. I say, "Thank You, God, that You never sleep and You are always watching over me. Thank You that You hear me anytime I pray!"

Sometimes I talk out loud

to God. But He also hears me when I pray in my **softest** whisper. He can **even** hear me when I talk silently to Him, when my words are **only in my head!**

When I say—**or think**—words like "Thank You, God!" or "Help me, God!" I can **always** be sure that **He hears them.** The Bible says that He does, and I believe His Word. I say, "Thank You, God, that You can **hear** me even when I am talking **softly,** even when I talk to You in my **mind.**"

Every time I pray, God listens to and accepts my prayer no matter what kind of prayer it is. I can pray a short prayer or a long prayer. I can pray a prayer I learned in Sunday school or church, or I can make up my own prayer. I can pray alone or with other people.

God says that praying with other people is very powerful. I can also pray for others, and I can ask them to pray for me. Sometimes everyone can pray together about something that is important to them. Praying for other people is one way I can share God's love with them. I say, "Dear God, help me pray for other people as often as I can!"

God watches over me and sees everything I do. He always wants me to do the right thing, but He still loves me even if I do something wrong. And no matter what, He always wants to hear from me.

If I talk to God about what I did wrong and tell Him I'm sorry, He is always happy to forgive me. He promises He will always forgive me if I ask Him to! And then He will help me learn to do the right thing. I say, "God, help me to always remember to obey my parents and to obey You too."

Jesus is God's Son. He came to earth so everyone could know more about God. When He was living on earth, Jesus talked to God too. He said that God loves little children very much and that they can always talk to God because they are special to Him.

Jesus told people, "If you ask anything in My name, I will do it." That's why I always end my prayers with the words "in Jesus' name I pray." This doesn't mean that God will always give me everything I ask for. But if it's something good He wants me to have, He will give it to me. I say, "Thank You, Jesus, for answering my prayers."

Each time I pray, I believe that God hears me and that He will answer my prayers. But I need to trust God to answer in His own way and whenever He wants to. Sometimes this is hard to do! Maybe someone special to me is sick, and I want them to get better right away. Or there's something I really want, and I don't like waiting for it.

It always helps to remember that my job is to pray. God's job is to answer my prayer. So I need to do my job and let God do His job. I say, "God, help me to wait patiently for You to answer my prayers."

I may be just a child, but my prayers have power because I am valuable to God. Even though children are small, their prayers are big in God's eyes. My prayers are so important to God that when I pray, He always comes closer to me. I like being close to God. That's why I talk to Him every day. I say, "Thank You, God, that You are close to me right now and You love to hear me pray."